My Princess Collection

Tiana

The Princess
and the Frog

Book Seven

Printed in China

First Edition

13 15 17 19 20 18 16 14 12

ISBN 978-1-4231-2571-6

T425-2382-5 12196

For more Disney Press fun,
visit www.disneybooks.com

Chapter One

One evening, Tiana and her friend Charlotte LaBouff were listening to Tiana's mother, Eudora, read a story about a frog that needed a kiss from a princess to turn him into a human prince.

Charlotte was ready to kiss a frog if it meant she could be a princess! But not so for Tiana! She would never kiss a frog. Yuck!

Back at home, Tiana and her father, James, talked of their dream of opening their own restaurant. Later, Tiana wanted to wish on the Evening Star so their dream would come true. James encouraged her to wish but also to remember to work hard—and never forget the importance of family and friends.

Chapter Two

The years went by and Tiana became a beautiful young woman. Her father had passed away, but Tiana was still determined to open their restaurant. She waited tables day and night and saved every spare penny she could.

Not far away, a carefree prince named Naveen arrived in town just in time for Mardi Gras. Tiana's friend Charlotte was especially excited to meet Prince Naveen at Big Daddy La Bouff's masquerade ball that night. "I'm going to need about 500 of your man-catching beignets," she told Tiana. Tiana was thrilled when Charlotte paid her. Now she had enough money to finally buy her restaurant!

That afternoon, Tiana made an offer on the old sugar mill that she and her father had picked out long ago. She imagined how glamorous the restaurant would look when it was done.

Meanwhile, downtown, a sinister figure named Dr. Facilier approached Prince Naveen and his valet, Lawrence. Dr. Facilier practiced evil voodoo, and he had wicked plans for the prince.

Lawrence didn't trust the stranger, but Naveen was intrigued and followed Facilier to a magic shop. Facilier told both men he could give them exactly what they wanted most, and he used a magic talisman to cast a spell.

Later, at the masquerade ball, Charlotte waited impatiently for her prince.

Just then, Prince Naveen arrived! But it wasn't really the prince at all. Dr. Facilier had magically transformed Lawrence so that he looked exactly like Naveen!

At the ball, Tiana discovered that someone had offered more money for the sugar mill. The deal was off!

Tiana wandered out to the balcony and looked up at the Evening Star. She closed her eyes and made a wish. When Tiana opened her eyes again, a frog was staring up at her.

Dr. Facilier had turned Prince Naveen into a frog, and Naveen thought that only a kiss from a princess could turn him back into a human. He also thought that Tiana was a princess. "Surely I could offer you some type of reward?"

Tiana felt sorry for the frog. Plus, she really did want her restaurant. She closed her eyes and— *SMOOCH!* Naveen was still a frog, but now Tiana was a frog, too!

Naveen and she grabbed on to some balloons and drifted to the bayou. That's where Naveen found out that Tiana was not a real princess.

Chapter Three

The next morning, Naveen and Tiana met a friendly, trumpet-playing alligator named Louis. He and Naveen talked about jazz music, but all Tiana cared about was finding someone to break the spell that had turned them into frogs.

Louis told them a magic woman named Mama Odie might be able to help. He agreed to take them to her. Maybe she would turn Louis into a human, too, and his dream of playing in a jazz band would finally come true!

While trying to catch a firefly for food, Tiana and Naveen accidentally tangled tongues and became stuck together. The firefly, named Ray, helped them and then kindly offered to show them the way to Mama Odie's.

On the way, Tiana prepared dinner for everyone. She asked Naveen to help, but he didn't know how. "When you live in a castle, everything is done for you," he said sadly.

Tiana gladly showed him how to prepare mushrooms for the gumbo. They laughed and joked as they cooked. The two frogs were starting to like each other.

Suddenly, scary shadows sent by the evil Dr. Facilier grabbed Naveen! Luckily, Mama Odie appeared just in time and saved him. Mama Odie was an old woman who used voodoo to help people. "We need to be human," Tiana told her.

Tiana peeked into Mama Odie's big pot of gumbo and saw an image of Big Daddy LaBouff as the king of Mardi Gras—which made Charlotte a princess! If Naveen could kiss "Princess" Charlotte before midnight, then he and Tiana would become human again!

Chapter Four

Tiana, Naveen, Louis, and Ray caught a ride on a riverboat back to the city. Along the way, Naveen confessed to Ray that he was in love with Tiana!

As they drifted along, Tiana pointed out the sugar mill she and her father had chosen for their restaurant many years ago. Naveen's heart sank. In order to make Tiana's dream come true, he would have to marry Charlotte and beg her to buy Tiana her restaurant.

Heartbroken, Naveen left Tiana. Just as he did, he was snatched up by the evil shadows!

Back at the LaBouff estate, the shadows swept in with Naveen. Facilier used him to restore the talisman's magic, and Lawrence changed into the handsome prince once again.

Naveen finally understood the wicked plot— just as Facilier locked him inside a small chest. Meanwhile, Ray told Tiana that Naveen was in love with her! Tiana was overjoyed. She felt the same way about Naveen. She raced to the parade to see if Naveen had kissed Charlotte yet. Instead, she saw Charlotte and the human Prince Naveen getting married! Not realizing that it was really Lawrence in disguise, Tiana was heartbroken.

Ray found Naveen and freed him from the chest. Just as Charlotte and her groom were about to say "I do," Naveen jumped onto Lawrence! The frog quickly pulled the talisman from the impostor's neck and tossed it to Ray.

In a different part of the parade, Louis was finally playing in a Mardi Gras jazz band! Just then Ray flew by, struggling with the heavy talisman. Louis knew what he had to do. He turned his back on the band and took off to help Ray.

Ray found Tiana and tossed her the talisman. Then Facilier knocked down the little bug and stepped on him!

Facilier quickly caught up with Tiana. Thinking fast, she threatened to shatter the talisman, but Facilier played a trick on her. Tiana magically found herself in her dream restaurant—and she was human again! "Don't forget your poor daddy," Facilier said, reminding her of her father's dream.

"My daddy never got what he wanted," Tiana declared. Suddenly she understood everything clear as day. "But he had what he needed." Her daddy knew that the love of his family was more important than anything else—that and the way he could cook and bring together people from all over to share food and good times.

Tiana shattered the talisman. Instantly, she was a frog again. Facilier lost control of the shadows, and all that was left of him was his hat.

Chapter Five

Tiana rushed to the church. There she overheard Naveen promise to marry Charlotte if she kissed him. "But you must give Tiana all the money she requires for her restaurant," said Naveen.

"Don't," Tiana protested, as she hopped out of the shadows. "My dream wouldn't mean anything without you." Charlotte knew true love when she saw it.

"I'll kiss you," she said to Naveen. "No marriage required!" But it was too late. The clock chimed midnight! Tiana and Naveen didn't mind. They were in love—even if they were still frogs.

17

Just then, Louis raced up. Crying, he held a
wounded Ray. Facilier had hurt him badly. Tiana
and Naveen raced to his side. Ray was happy to see
that his friends were together and in love. Then his
light flickered out.

Returning to the bayou, the friends bid the
little firefly good-bye. They were sad until they
looked up at the Evening Star. Next to it was
another bright star—a star that no one had ever
seen before.

Chapter Six

A little while later, Naveen and Tiana were
married by Mama Odie in the bayou. As Naveen
kissed Tiana, something truly magical happened:
the frogs turned back into humans!

"Like I told you, kissing a princess breaks the
spell!" Mama Odie said with a laugh.

"And once you became my wife . . . that made
you—" Naveen began.

"A princess," Tiana finished. "You just kissed
yourself a princess!"

Soon there was a new restaurant in town—Tiana's Palace. It was the best place to go for good food, lively music, and fun with friends and family.

Tiana had nothing more to wish for, because she had everything she'd ever wanted—and everything she needed.